The Perfect Love Story!

The 1999 *The Guardian*/Piccadilly writing competition for teenagers, *The Perfect Love Story?* inspired some excellent work. The panel of judges, consisting of Andrew Motion (Poet Laureate, Professor of Creative Writing at the University of East Anglia), Joanna Carey (reviewer and feature writer for *The Guardian*) and Liz Fraser (presenter, BBC Live and Kicking, Friday) chose ten winning stories from over a thousand entries. These winning stories, by Emma Bevin, Louise Coutts, Oliver Emanuel, Jennifer Morrison, Amy Pragnell, Rebecca Prestwich, Sally Roe, Freya Scott, Marianka Swain and Jason Walsh, display refreshing originality, humour and diversity. They capture love in its myriad forms in a memorable collection, revealing the creative talent of today's young writers.

The Perfect Love Story!

Winners of
The Guardian/Piccadilly
teenage writing competition

Piccadilly Press • London

Set in Justlefthand and Meridien

Printed and bound by WBC, Bridgend
for the publishers Piccadilly Press Ltd,
5 Castle Road, London NW1 8PR

A catalogue record for this book is available
from the British Library

ISBNs: 1 85340 529 9 (hardback)
1 85340 524 8 (trade paperback)

1 3 5 7 9 10 8 6 4 2

Design by Louise Millar
Cover design by Judith Robertson

Contents

Foreword

Andrew Motion

Judging this competition, although often a (properly) testing task, was also fun and rewarding. The overall standard was high – and when the entries were good, they were very good.

I found myself wanting to reward stories that were off the beaten track, and I think my fellow judges – Joanna Carey of *The Guardian*, and Liz Fraser of 'Live and Kicking, Friday' – felt the same way. Although our views didn't coincide in every case, we were broadly in agreement.

When the fog of adolescence blows in, it's often difficult for a young writer to maintain the clarity and sense of surprise that most children possess. And the subject of love – let alone of perfect love – is especially likely to lead to self-consciousness and embarrassed clichés. Given these things, our shortlisted writers in general, and our final ten in particular, did very well. Congratulations to them all; this book contains a rich mix of new talent.

Andrew Motion

Chamber Street

Emma Bevin

Chamber Street

Dear Nick,

Last night I took a can of Coke and a packet of crisps, and went down to Chamber Street for the first time in nine years. I swung myself up on the church wall, and snuggled up in the corner, where the stones are worn smooth by a hundred similar bums, and looked around.

The first time I sat there was with you in 1984. I wrote it in my diary: *June 23rd, 1984. Spent the whole Saturday afternoon with Nick.* It was a gloriously sunny day, and the windows of the church winked and blinked at passers-by. The pathway up to the church was clear of weeds, and the grass was kept short. Generations and generations lay sleeping in the afternoon heat beneath the shelter of the giant yew tree that grew there. Despite the finicky tidiness of the sexton, the whole place had an atmosphere, of peace, unlike the cemetery down the road, where the graves are in regimented rows and no one would ever dare sit on the wall. The gravestones were irregular and lopsided. It's a funny place to go with your boyfriend, a graveyard, but it never felt morbid.

When I had finished my Coke, I wandered over to the church itself. I walked over to where the Norman tower casts a shadow at five o'clock in the evening, and thought about salty, smoky kisses in the privacy of the ancient stone.

I went into the porch of the church, where the remains of Catholic murals had been recovered from the Puritan whitewash. I sat down next to a pair of wellies, some dirt and a spider, and thought how romantic the place had once been. How refreshingly cool it was in the summer, and how the vicar had frowned at us as he swept out of the church, disgusted by modern youth.

Next, I got up, and walked out of the church and graveyard, and wandered into Chamber Street. I can trace our whole life through that street. Carry on reading and live it back with me, please.

First the record store. Remember how that funny little bloke who ran the shop really liked Duran Duran and it was always their posters that adorned the shop window? I still think that you looked like John Taylor, no matter what you say. Do you remember how you used to take the mickey out of me something rotten when I bought one of Duran Duran's records? I never had a problem with you buying Madonna.

The place was an odd shape, remember? I have never seen a round record store since. It was good though, with the black carpet, and the red rug in the middle to look like an old LP. Couldn't you buy magazines there, the music ones that you couldn't get anywhere else?

I could talk about that odd little place for ever, but now I shall go on to talk about the café. You know, your mum's friend Mrs Bunton ran it, that big lady. It was so embarrassing when you burst into a fit of giggles when she fell over the uneven floor and landed on her face in a cream cake she'd dropped. She knew you laughed at her. The only reason she didn't chuck you out was because you were such a good customer. Oh, can you remember the juke-box, the really old one that played those awful country-and-western records, that stood in the corner? You couldn't see how tatty it was because of the awful lighting in there. Uneven floor, bad lighting, awful music, why did we go there? The cream cakes, I suppose. They really were something worth getting excited about, weren't they?

The next place I'll move on to is Wedding Belles. If I'm tracing our lives I should have mentioned this place nearer the end, but as it was next to the café, it makes sense to write about it now. Let's see. You proposed on Christmas Day of '84. And the week before we'd popped into the record store for our copy of Band Aid's single. Well, it seemed only right that you should propose to me close to a church, next to a shop full of wedding dresses. I loved looking in that shop. I'm really glad my dress came from there.

Although the woman who owned the place gave me the creeps, with her constant scowl and the way she insisted she was *Ms*, not *Miss*. Odd woman. It was another odd-shaped shop, too, wasn't it? And as far as I can remember, the walls were covered with pictures of weddings and certificates. Maybe you don't want to hear about weddings. I'll move on.

Now we come to the car accessory shop. The Motor Way. I suppose it was convenient for you and Dad, as it was right opposite the garage, but did you have to drag me in there every week to discuss my car with that slimy little bloke in charge? It always smelled funny in there. I still can't place what it smelled of, can you? And there was that awful calendar of page three models, not to mention the other pin-ups. Ah well, that's not important now, is it?

The final part of our journey is the garage. Yes, my Dad's business, where I earned pocket money on Saturdays, where you worked all of our life. Sitting here at my desk, I don't even have to close my eyes to visualise it. As I walked down the street, I kept my eyes to the ground, only looking up to where it used to be when I was right in front of it. I don't know why it hurt most to look there. Perhaps it was because I half expected to see you, stripped down to the waist, hands resting on some old car, staring thoughtfully into the open bonnet, oil all in your blond highlights and coating your jeans. And I also half expected to see my dad come wandering out of the 'office' to see me, yelling at you to clean up before you came to meet me.

If my memory is correct, the collection of bits of building that had been cobbled together over the years to form the place had resulted in something more resembling a bomb-site than an efficient business. Bags of tools and bits of engines, cans of petrol and oil, and the odd door, the odd 'souvenir', bits of indescribable junk, all thrown together in a filthy jumble also added to the 'character' of the place, shall we say? Bins of rags, piles of boiler suits, and buckets on the floor in heavy rainstorms when the roof leaked and my dad would send you up to patch it up. Out the back was the pump. You used to get so cross having to pump for water. I don't blame you, though, especially as you had to wash there yourself.

The office sticks in my mind. When Dad retired, and we took over the business, I thought I got it quite respectable. I didn't have the heart to get rid of the old till, though – at least we agreed on something there.

What I remember most from being a little girl and going in there, was the big desk. Anything like that's fascinating to a little kid, and I was really struck by it. All the drawers full of pens, most of which didn't work, and bits of newspapers and receipts, and even the odd treasure, like the ring Dad bought for Mum for her fiftieth, and then lost for three years. That was in there, along with the account books – big, red leather-bound volumes I used to flick through.

Surely you haven't forgotten how you would leave love-letters in the drawers for me? Or perhaps you have. Mum used to do the same for Dad, but, as he was always messier than me, he lost them before he'd even found them, if you know what I mean. Most of them were found when I turned the whole place out in '88, when we took over.

And so that's it. We've reached the end of the street. Turning round and looking back through the jumble of buildings that made up the street, we would sometimes comment on how pretty the church looked as the sun sank, and the sky turned pink, and you would slide your arm round my shoulders, your face blotting out the sunset, your lips blotting out any talk about the church. Can you remember?

But of course everything changes. Nine years ago, they knocked down Chamber Street, flattened all the funny little shops, the garage, the café, and put up a lot of little brick boxes. None of the boxes have gardens, or character. The only way you can tell them apart is the pattern on the net curtains. The people who wander around in the sunset are not people I know. I can't place the Nissan Micra and the green Mini that are parked beside each other outside two of the boxes. Walking up and down the street I feel like crying, but not with all those net-curtained eyes watching me. Yet if I close my own eyes, I can still picture my long, muscly mechanic with oil in his highlights, coming out of the record store with a Madonna LP under his arm.

The church is still there, of course, although the grass has grown long, and the gate creaks and hangs at a funny angle. Before I left Chamber Street, I walked back to the place where we met, where we kissed, where we married – and slid inside the door, and dropped down on a pew. The place is bare of flowers, your mother must have given up the flower-arranging, which is a shame.

I was sat there a long time, and it was only when a new vicar – much younger than the one who used to glower at us before he married us – breezed in that I walked out. He smiled, before wandering on closer to the altar and sitting down himself. It's funny how everything changes.

You live at one end of England, I live at the other. I had thought that Chamber Street, stuck roughly in the middle of us, would remain the same. But it didn't. Whether there are people scattered around who remember Nick and Amanda's wedding, I don't know. Perhaps I shall go back to the town this evening and see if I bump into anyone. Then tomorrow, I shall go home, back to Bournemouth.

If you have read this far down the letter, then perhaps you would be interested enough to give me a ring sometime.

Amanda

Perfect Love

Louise Coutts

Perfect Love

Kaya sat in the open air, allowing herself to be hypnotised by the quivering red flames in front of her. In the fire's depth she saw antelope springing from the embers, yellow jungle spirits dancing and hopping with the orange nymphs, all in the silence of her village at midnight.

She found it hard to sleep in the dry season. The floating dust caught her throat and she woke, coughing. Kaya watched her village in the moonlight; shadow to shadow, she knew it all by heart and felt safe and protected by the circle of huts.

The wind tossed up her hair and played with it in the cool breeze. Kaya liked the wind, the way it carried everything – sounds, smells, fortune and danger. She alerted all her senses and waited for what the wind had to offer her that night.

She heard jungle bats, clapping their wings as they met up in the night, crickets trying in vain to make music like the birds, but failing miserably. Then a foreign sound, a stranger, met her ear – the earth was thundering from the direction where the sun died each night. It was not a sound of the earth, it was a machine.

Kaya had learned of machines from the whitemen

with coloured helmets who constantly harassed her village with their bulldozers and lorries, trying to convince her people that their village space would be far more beneficial as a group of compound villas for big oil tycoons from overseas.

Their last visit ended in a quarrel between her father and the whiteman with the yellow helmet.

Now they had returned, as promised, determined to get 'planning permission'.

Quickly remembering what she had been taught, Kaya sprung to her feet to alert her father. When he appeared his face frightened Kaya. The fear and dread of losing his village to the whitemen showed in his eyes. They glistened in the darkness. The other men of the village were gathering wives, children and possessions as best they could in the moonlight.

Her father turned to Kaya and said, 'Remember what to do, Kaya?' His eyes focused on her trembling pupils. 'Run through the night, through the day if you have to, just keep running until the danger is past, do you hear me?'

'Yes, Father,' was the answer that came from a muffled mouth covered by a sleeve soaked in tears. With that her father kissed her, then nudged her gently, setting her off on her long marathon of escape.

Totally disoriented by the darkness, Kaya ran through plains and marshes unknown to her, until her feet had gone numb with fatigue. She wandered aimlessly, looking for a sheltered, desolate spot for her to waste away the remaining night without her father. Ahead of her, as though illuminated by the moon, stood a tree, tilting to the side from the wind. There she sat awake, listening to the familiar, yet foreign sounds of her new orphanage home.

Kaya had always felt pity for those who were alone. She thought it was one of the worst things in the world to be unloved, not remembered, not even noticed by anyone else. She had never had a mother. In her mind the only person who had any value to her was her father, and now that he was gone, she was alone. She began to feel sorry for herself.

The sun pulled itself over the horizon and woke Kaya gently. She sat up, alarmed by the brightness of an outdoor awakening. She had no time to take in the new scenery that met her hazy eyes before she was lunged upon by a creature. A dog. Kaya was terrified, she had never seen a wolf up close and did not plan to make it a ritual. Drool settled on her face like dew and paws stroked her clammy, damp skin. She screamed and soon a man, nearly as dark as she was, but quite obviously white, shadowed her figure and pulled the beast off its new-found toy.

'I am terribly sorry, my dear . . . You see, Willie gets quite lonely in the garden by himself. I'm sure he didn't mean to startle you!'

Kaya was confused. He was a whiteman but spoke her tongue. Normally the men with the coloured helmets simply shouted at her father, as though he couldn't hear, never mind understand what was being said.

The man smiled and helped her to her feet. In her mind, she wondered whether he counted as a whiteman if he spoke her language. Her father had ordered her that she was never to speak to a white-man, that they would always take what was not rightfully theirs and harm anyone that got in their way.

The man's soft eyes smiled too. He gestured to her to take his hand, which was too close to the dog for Kaya's liking. Even so, she took it and when her hand was placed on the dog's back she didn't scream. She liked the dog's fur, soft and silky, like none of the creatures her father had ever brought back to the village, dead or alive. It was a feeling that she wanted to hold on to, not to give back to the man who could smile with his eyes.

He noticed her reluctance to leave Willie, and started to walk slowly, hoping that she would follow and walk with him a while.

As they walked, he learned of the troubles of Kaya's village, and how she came to be, as it happened, on his estate. She learned that he was indeed a whiteman, who had come to Africa to study bats and had long ago retired to the villa, probably built by those persecuting Kaya's village. He, an ageing man of fifty or more, was intrigued by the small, delicate child, who ate every word he told her, as though he was reciting an old fable passed down through the vines of generations. As it was obvious to anyone that this child was alone, he thought it best to invite her back to his home where he could care for her until the time came for her to leave, for whatever reason it may be.

Once inside his rich, whitewashed dwellings, Kaya felt a stranger, an intruder in another culture, and felt obliged to leave. She turned towards the door and caught his eye. His face was no longer smiling, it reminded her of her father's before she left the village. She could tell that this man had always been alone, apart from his dog who Kaya did not think of as a substitute for human affection. She knew that somewhere out in the wilderness was her father, with a heart broken by the loss of his daughter. She did not think it was right to do the same thing to another man, so she stayed.

She stayed through her youth and her woman-hood. At the age of thirty she was immensely pleased with her life; she had a nice home where she was now a deep-rooted part. However, this was a trifle of the emotion held by the man. He adored Kaya, not to hold, more to watch. When cleaning, when singing, he craved every inch of her. He had never been a romantic man and she knew nothing of passion or sex. To her, the best feelings she had ever felt were for him.

They drifted through the years, talking, listening and often simply observing each other. They knew each other by heart and by soul. He would read to her and she would revert back to her childhood and swallow each word, with her devotion to his voice. Their relationship satisfied the needs of both parties and left them both more besotted with each other than before. Kaya needed him as a friend, someone without authority, yet not as naïve and uncultured as herself. He needed her as the woman in his life, to love and cherish, without the normal obligatory demands of romance.

They lived each day together, worshipping their lives together and privately praying that the day would never come when they would be separated, be it by death or society.

Throughout the years of their companionship no one ever visited the house – they had no cause to. Food was fresh from the garden and the postal service only operated in the town thirty miles away. They were isolated for a lifetime's worth of each other. Had a contact been made with an outside source, trouble would have arisen. Both whitemen and village society disapproved of relationships outside certain boundaries, which the man and Kaya had crossed decades before, under the tree tilting to the side from the wind. Therefore they shared everything alone, just the two of them, the seasons passing, the drought, the thunderstorms and eventually his death.

Kaya buried his body near the tree, tilting to the side from the wind. She was silent, she never wept or moaned. She never said goodbye. In her mind they lived on together, he still told her stories and she swallowed his words, like before. In her mind they lived on and on, they lived their perfect love.

Let's Skip

Oliver Emanuel

Let's Skip

My name is Damian, 'cos (according to my muma) I was 'hell to produce'. And though I admit to being no Albert E and a bit of a clumsy-clots at times, I am always ready to do my bit. I clean the plates and knives and forks and spoons and bowls, I iron our clothes, I do our washing and drying, I make Muma breakfast and lunch and tea, I make sure she is comfortable (with big fluffy pillows under her neck and a good video to watch with her tea) and I have even hoovered when required. (I have to do all this on account of Muma being poorly and not at all in the best of bodies.) Muma and me is alone, as my dad left Muma when she was ripe with me and I just a twinkle. (I cannot say as how I miss him, my muma being parent enough for anyone.)

I work in a fast-food restaurant where we do chickens and chips and stuff. I work there on week-days and on Sunday afternoons when dogs and children go out for walks with mumas and dads. I am a packer. In fact, I am *the* packer. Maureen (who is the server) presses buttons (which I'm not supposed to touch) when the customer says their order and small greeny writing appears on the screen (like 'Regular Chicken Meal One') and I pack the chicken and chips into a cardboard box. It is quite hard work as there is no seat on which to perch, but when there are loads of customers it doesn't matter because you haven't time to dawdle. I get paid three pounds sixty-nine pence an hour (double on Sundays) which I get every Friday from Jon (the fat manager) with a white slip with my name on. (I have to show Muma the money as soon as I get home, and she writes a list of things I am to get in the week, like shopping and toilet rolls.)

I like working at the fast-food restaurant as it means I can think a lot. I think when I fry the chips (two and a half minutes in the fryer with the fat in) and when I pack the chicken. I don't talk as it can make the order wrong and customers don't like that, so I am given plenty of ticks just to think in my noodle. What do I think about? Circles, mainly, or Picasso, or Muma (or even Julia). I like circles, most especially drawing them with pencils (nice and thick) over big pieces of paper, circle upon circle, all different kinds of circles, tall and small and thin and fat and perfect and smudged. Dr Scott said I was to draw as it 'helps concentration and gives expression to grievances', which I don't really understand but don't mind because I enjoy it. I think of Picasso most when I am on chips, and I can play with each little potato-sword, placing them here and there to make a person or a chair or a dancer, his dancer being my favourite one, with the feet kicking and the arms stretched (like she is really dancing).

But most often I think of Muma.

I can see her cough-cough-coughing in her bed with no cup of tea or pillow-fluffer and I worry. I know that it should not be me that worries about her but she that should worry about me, but when she is so poorly it hardly seems rainbow-fair. I worry much the whole time. She can't walk any more and we have no phone with which she could call an ambulance. As to the particulars of her poorliness I haven't the faintest, and anyway I 'wouldn't understand' (says she). But not knowing is worse, and I know so little that I am much much worse than any normal bod, I don't know anything and worry my noodle off completely. But I don't let her know. My muma's always said that I was a brave boy, and a brave boy I have to be. What with Muma unable to sleep 'cos of the pain and her head thump-thumping all day long and her crying into her duvet all night (so as not to wake me), I have to be brave and not show her that I worry. Oh yes, with her I am nice and breezy and kind to her poor ears.

But while I pack, I do worry.

I also get to look at people, which is one of my favourite things. They are often the same people every week at the same time on the same day, but it is fun to pre-pack their order before Maureen's till flashes green, and so look cool and froody, handing over the food pronto. I look at people's noses first ('cos noses make me laugh in my head) and then at their eyes. Eyes is very strange as there are so many different colours (blue, green, black, grey, brown, hazel), almost every person has a different colour, and colour is what I like. Looking at people's clothes and I know when I should hurry and pack quick or when I can take my time a smidgen. (Blokes with big, puffy jackets who look all surly have to be packed up double time.) I have perfected a certain sideways flicker, which I do when I reach across to the plastic bags on my left, and this flicker allows me to see the whole person's face completely without them seeing me looking. I used to stare at people when I started, but Maureen gave me a clip and said I was to 'stop gawpin'.' (I don't like Maureen much as she is bossy and only small but with a high whiny voice.)

It is Monday. The slugs are out, the autumn damp is beginning. The time is five to twelve.

I am sitting after preparing for the day ahead (chips and chicken at the ready) on the floor by the staff door. The restaurant is not open yet and I sit and wait while Jon and Andrew (the cook) finish getting ready. I look down at the whitey-beige tiles of the floor, as there is very little else to look at – there is nothing to see inside this place. Jon and Andrew are making a lot of noise with pans. What's the matter, I wonder?

– Hey, you two, I holla, what is all the curfuffle?

– Late again, mutters Andrew pertly, late a-bloody-gain.

– Late? Who's late? I ask (as I cannot remember who is on duty this particular Monday).

– Lady Julia Muck, says Jon with a frown, your girlfriend.

My face turns all stupid and pink and I lowers my eyes to the floor.

I can't stand it when Jon calls her that, anything but *that*. Anyway, we aren't. We aren't together or anything. We're just friends. That's it. Girls don't interest me. I like circles and Picasso and Muma.

– I don't have any time for girls. Girls are sillier than sausages.

I'm lying.

Jon knows I'm lying.

Andrew knows I'm lying.

They smile and high-eyebrow each other and turn back to their work, stifling giggles.

– Bugger off, the pair of you, I say in my most menacing voice. They both shut up as I am six foot two and quite wide. But as I turn to retreat to the front counter there is a swish as the door is opened, and in she steps.

No one would say that Julia was beautiful. She is

short (five foot four) and thin, with quite a pretty face and a nice friendly smile. (She also has nice curves in what I believe to be the right places, but since the only pictures I see are on the TV and in Picasso, I haven't much to go on.) *I* think she is the most beautiful person I ever saw. She isn't just nice-looking, but she is a nice person: always nice to the customers and nice to her parents and nice to her friends; and she is nice to me. I remember the first day she arrived. She came in and asked Maureen for an application form. I gawped. Her voice was so soft and kind, and her dark brown eyes were deep and circly and I gawped. Maureen clouted me round the ear and told me to 'find an application form in the office, fool.' She was lovely. No one would say that Julia was beautiful, except me.

– Hiya, gorgeous, says Julia, looping an arm round my ample waist and squeezing tight.

–Hullo, babe, I chirp, giving her light brown hair a peck with my lips.

This is the moment that, if I had been a good soldier and am with St Peter and all his angels, I would ask to be held. In Julia's arms I feel like a lion, a king, a teddy bear. I forget everything around me and the sky and the grass and the people altogether, and I'm held freeze-frame in happiness. Her body is warm and soft, her bosoms press against my chest and I ache with warmness. I'm not totally sure of what sex is exactly (I know it makes babies and that it is for a husband and wife to 'join as one') but I just want to melt warmful into Julia. I can't hold her tight enough, I can't kiss her light brown hair enough, I want her warmness and smell. That's the other thing she does: smell beautiful. It's like apples and oranges and sugar all mixed up to form one lovely dinner of a smell. The smell is her smell: somehow the combination of moisturiser and scent is her exactly. Perfect.

– If you two love-birds have quite finished, there are customers to be fried, gruffed Jon from the kitchen.

Julia and me suddenly snaps apart and my heaven is broken. Julia walks through the kitchen and into the small back office and removes her coat. Jon says to me, 'Damian, you soft bastard, go and get some chips from the freezer downstairs or you won't have enough for the two o'clock rush.'

– Damo and Julie up a tree, K-I-S-S-I-N-G, sings Andrew, brandishing an uncooked chicken leg. I go to him, grab the chicken and throw it at his apron, he gropes for it, catches hold of it and smiles – calm down, lad, calm down.

– I'll calm you if you don't shut it, blurt I.

– Promises, promises, tuts Andrew.

– Fucking poof, says I. (Andrew is indeed a poof and sees a bloke called Hank from the local supermarket. Muma says they should be burned at the stake, but Julia says that they are just normal people who like the same-gender normal people. He does get on my tits though, homo-jokes aside.)

I descend the stairs next to the office and open the big walk-in freezer. I fumble around the pebble-like beans and grab up two big boxes of chips. I feel a hand touch my shoulder.

– Andrew, I'm going to knock you into next Tuesday, I says, turning round.

– You can knock me into any Tuesday you like, sexy.

It's Julia. She grabs my thick neck and, tiptoey, leans her lips towards me. I love her. These little things, like her surprising me with kisses, are what I love. 'The kiss is a strange and wonderful thing' said a bloke off TV, and it is indeed wonderful and indeed a little strange. Why we humans would want to push our burp-holes, grubbins or whatever at each other is a very strange notion indeed. But I love it. Soft and wet and warm. Yum.

– HURRYUPYOUSOPPYBASTARDS.

– All right, all right, I yell up the stairs, gently disengaging myself from Julia. I turn and umph-up the chips from the freezer floor. As I bend down Julia pinches my bum. We giggle as we ascend the stairs into the kitchen.

Julia is very good at serving. She is always very p and q and her little fingers dart over the buttons like a piano-penguin over ivories. In fact, the whole operation is like a mini orchestra from the telly, each of us playing our part: Julia, singing out quick repetitive tunes to customers and conducting us with her green flashy baton; me, beating regular time with the chips and the chicken and the box and the bag, bom bom bom, and occasionally tooting 'TRAY' when I need more chicken; Andrew with a swish and a swish, and a dip and a dip, preparing the chicken, and a wipe and a wiping-ready the friers and cleaning up afterwards; and Jon trumpeting 'bloody-move-ons', pushing and pulling the whole box of thuds into a harmonical chicken-tune. It may seem silly, but there is enough music in even the dullest of jobs.

Today went slowly. Not enough customers to keep us busy, and too many to sit around and chat. Julia worked well with getting all the money and orders right, and I worked quick as I could to complete everything in the proper two minutes (a stupid rule, invented by Jon to make us work quicker). We didn't get much chance to chat, except to exchange news about our parents: her muma having a cold; and she (like always) enquiring about Muma. Sometimes Julia comes round our house to see Muma and make her soup and stuff, while I'm at work, and Muma really likes that, and Muma really likes Julia too, but always says to me how she is 'too good for a scruff' like me. I *am* a bit of a scruff. But Julia seems not to mind.

Love creeped to me so slowly – I didn't realise it until it kissed me on the lips. Julia had always been so special to me, so kind and considerate to me, but I never dreamed of feeling anything for another person except my muma. And although now I still love Muma, it is a different love from the feelings I have for Julia. My tummy is all churny and twisty when I think I won't see her, and even when I know I'll see her my tummy squirls around. I have always loved Muma: I don't think there was ever a point I doubted it. But to feel love come upon you slowly, with every word and giggle and sigh and hello and goodbye and movement of the fingers and look and blink and laugh and every single sight and touch, is an amazing experience indeed. Maureen says she doesn't believe in love, that it is just some kind of label (like on jam), but that simply shows that she has never been in love before. Not properly, at least. (Which is sad because she has been married for twenty-one years and has two kids.) When you are in love you don't dare blaspheme, don't question its value because, just maybe, maybe it will go, and for it to go would be a truly bad and drogritty thing to happen.

Julia and me is finished at six o'clock on the dot, with the night staff arriving at five to. Julia collects her coat from the office, and I collect my jacket from downstairs, and we leave together. Holding hands.

The autumn has toddled forward early, and the night is upon us already. The street lamps sit like bright oranges in a black fruit bowl as we cross at the lights near my house, us dawdling as much as possible so as to waste time. Julia's hand is soft and warm, and her tiny fingers disappear in my huge gorilla-podges.

– Let's skip, says Julia, and she starts dancing up the road. I join in, but don't want to as I know that Muma and the house are close.

Julia and Muma are in different worlds. Julia really lives only down the end of Grosvenor Road (two minutes' walk), but that is not my thingy. Julia is so bouncy and soft and warm and skips, while Muma is still and hard and cold and is dying. One is life and lives, the other is death and dies. I know that for me, life will not end with Muma but will probably continue just two minutes' walk away.

We stand at the steps to my house. Julia looks up to the second floor and the little slip of light that snakes through the drawn curtain.

I know the change will be difficult for me. I love Muma. (All of her, from her demands for pillow-fluffing and tea to the way she kisses me goodnight on my left cheek, always the left cheek.) Yes, I know the change will be difficult for me. Perhaps it will be harder for Julia as I have not really asked her if she would mind the company of a six foot two oaf who can hoover. But it will not be hard for Muma. That pain will be saved from her. At least. There will be no more tears or pills needed for that pain. When she goes, I will go. Yet she will not see me leave. She will not see me leave my key behind and not look back as I walk down the road.

Eternity Is As Long As It Lasts

Jennifer Morrison

Eternity Is As Long As It Lasts

You know when you meet that person. You know –
THE ONE. The one you fall in love with at first sight,
and you'll love no matter what – wherever they go
or whatever they do.

Sounds corny, doesn't it? But it does happen. It
happened to Joel and me. The house two doors away
had been deserted for around three years. I never
thought it would be bought by anyone. Eventually,
though, it was, and after watching dozens of people
walk in and out of the house, the 'For Sale' was covered with a 'Sold' sign, and a removal van arrived
outside. The family who moved in consisted of a man
and a woman who were around forty years old, and
two younger boys who were, we found out later,
fourteen and nineteen. The younger boy was Joel
and the older was David.

They moved in, and after a few days my mum
went round to invite the man and woman around
for a drink. She came back with a huge smile on her
face and told us that their names were Phoebe and
Brian. Apparently, she and Phoebe had liked each
other instantly.

Joel quickly made friends with the boys down our
road, but I never thought that he fitted in properly.

He was friendly and caring and welcoming to people, which none of the other boys were.

Pretty soon, I developed an enormous crush on him, as apart from being a nice person, he was very good-looking. I was delighted when he turned up at my house to ask me if I wanted to go to the woods with him and his friends. We walked over there together to meet his friends who were playing football on the park behind the trees.

We started talking and I found myself telling him about school and friends, and I found him really easy to talk to. We never actually met up with his friends, we just kept on walking, and we got to the bench on the side of the gardens. It's really high up there, and we could see all the way over to Birmingham. It was really romantic, as the sun was just setting and the sky was orange and pink. It was there that it happened. My first kiss. I don't know how or why it happened, but I'm glad it did, and it left my body tingling, and I walked home in a daze. Before we got back to my house, he asked me, 'Jennie, will you go out with me?' I was so happy, I said, 'Yes, of course I will.' I don't know how he gathered the nerve to ask me, boys of his age don't generally ask girls of my age out. That was just the sort of person he was, spoke his mind, and I knew then that it was love at first sight.

Over the next few weeks, we saw quite a lot of

each other, but when we weren't together I missed him more than I had ever missed anyone before. I knew that I loved him, but I couldn't share it with anyone, because they would just tell me that it was a silly crush.

I was helping his mum paint their hallway that special afternoon. We were going to paint it blue and white like the sky, and then she was going to paint the borders with rainbow colours. He walked in with a triumphant smile on his face, because Aston Villa had beaten Liverpool in the match he had just been to. He wanted to celebrate, so his mum told me to go home and change out of my old clothes while she packed a picnic. It was a warm July afternoon, so I changed into my shorts and T-shirt, not giving a thought to what I looked like.

When I got back to their house, having told my dad where I was going, Joel was ready and waiting for me. We decided to go back to our bench at the top of the hill.

While we ate, we talked about school and other things, and Joel told me how his friends thought he was really weird going out with a younger girl. I asked him if he was bothered about it, and he said, 'If it had bothered me, I wouldn't have asked you to begin with. Anyway, I'm glad it was you rather than anyone else. I love you.'

I was surprised. This didn't happen to people of

my age, that I was aware of, but then I realised that I didn't actually care what anyone else thought. 'I love you too,' I told him.

He laughed, but sounded relieved. 'Thank God for that,' he said. 'I thought that you'd think that I was weird, too.'

'Never,' I told him. 'You're the only one who understands me, isn't put off the first time I open my mouth, and doesn't care what I look like.'

I lay back on the grass, staring at the clouds in the sky. He lay beside me, holding my hand and pointing out the clouds that looked like objects. It felt just right lying there, with him, and nothing in the world to worry us. I didn't care about anything, I just enjoyed being with Joel.

We had other afternoons just like that throughout the summer holidays, but we never went back to that place. Joel said that it was special and we should save it. He gave me a necklace, with an emblem of two dolphins swimming together. I still have it, but don't wear it because it hurts too much to be reminded of him.

At the end of the holidays, Joel went to France and I went to Scotland with some family and friends. Everyone teased me about being split from my 'other half'. Joel always made a point of coming round to meet my family, and I think they understood how close we were and they approved of him.

When I got home, there was a package from him. I didn't open it straight away – I left it in the mail rack and ran round to their house to see him. I hadn't seen David's little Fiesta, but I'd seen their big car parked, so I knew someone must be in.

I couldn't wait to see Joel – I missed him so much it ached! I also wanted to give him his present – a heart engraved with two 'J's, which hung on a chain. I knew that he wouldn't think it was stupid.

I knew something was wrong when Phoebe opened the door to me. She usually had so much energy that she ran to the door and flung it open, but today, she walked and opened it really slowly, as if she had been dreading my visit.

She looked so sad. Her face was red – especially round the eyes. Her clothes were crumpled and her hair was a mess. She looked at me and said, 'He's not here,' so quietly that I almost didn't hear.

'What do you mean? Where is he?' I asked. I hadn't meant to sound aggressive, but it came out so fast that I couldn't help it.

'He's dead,' she said, before bursting into tears. I didn't believe her, or didn't want to, and I just stood there staring at this distraught woman, who I knew so well.

She managed to stop herself after a few moments, and she pulled me through the door and into their kitchen. She busied herself making coffee and put a cup down in front of me. Then she sat down on the other side of the table. 'How?' I asked, not quite believing that it was true. Phoebe seemed to have gathered herself, and just managed to get the words out.

'David was bringing him home from his gran's the other night. They'd stopped at some traffic lights, and a drunk driver crashed into them. David had a few cracked ribs and a broken leg, but Joel was killed immediately.'

She reached across the table to hold my hand, but I pulled it away. I didn't want anyone to touch me except Joel. I knew then that he was dead and I would never see him again.

Slowly, I reached into my pocket and pulled out the necklace, placed it on the table and walked out of their house. I heard Phoebe pick it up and start to sob all over again.

I didn't cry until I reached my room, and then I couldn't stop. I kept remembering his smiling face and him telling me that he loved me.

I spent two days in there, not eating or drinking or letting anyone in to talk to me. I felt like I wanted to die, too. Phoebe managed eventually to get me out. She told me that I was being selfish, and that she wanted me to sing at his funeral. I knew I couldn't go on like I had been doing, and I let her in.

Joel was buried on the second of September, 1995. I couldn't get myself to go to his funeral. Everyone seemed to understand when I came downstairs not wearing the clothes that they had planned for me. I knew I couldn't sing for him if he wasn't there. It seemed pointless. To me, I would only be drawing in the guests and relations, inviting them to ask me questions about Joel, questions that I couldn't answer without bursting into tears.

Instead, I went to our special place. Before I left our empty house, I remembered his package. I took it from where I had left it, and walked over to the woods and park to our bench.

While I sat there, I remember wishing that he would come and slip his arms round my waist and tell me that it was OK, that he wasn't dead, that it was all a big mistake and that he loved me and wouldn't leave me on my own. But that sort of thing only happens in films. Instead, I sat alone in the silence. It was odd not to see people around there. It seemed that the world was giving a small tribute to Joel. Most of the people on the street had gone to say their final goodbye at his funeral. I didn't want to say goodbye.

I took out the package. There was a picture of a French villa, it was beautiful, the sort of place everyone wants to live. He had written on the back, *This is where our children will live.*

His letter was short:

Dear Jennie,

I'm having fun here, but I miss you! We'll be home soon, though, and we'll be together. I want to ask you a question that is easier to write than say. I love you and think I always will. Please be my girlfriend for ever. One day we'll get married and keep each other happy for ever.

Please say yes. This is the most serious I have ever been about anyone.

All my love,

JOEL

PS I'll be back a bit earlier than planned. Gran's ill again.

I looked inside the envelope. It contained an eternity ring. I have always wondered how long eternity is. It doesn't mean for ever. It means 'as long as it lasts'.

When something like this happens to you, you always look for a reason. Usually there isn't one. You have to realise that you should enjoy life while you have it, and knowing Joel has shown me that you can enjoy life. If you let it be enjoyable. I didn't until a long time after he died. I didn't and couldn't sleep properly. I always saw him. He haunts me. I often see the car he was in, just before the other one hit it. I wasn't there, but I can picture it. I can never stop it happening. You have to take what life deals you. Unfortunately, this is what life dealt me.

I know that it was true love. I also know that the saying 'only the good die young' is true. Joel is the best thing that ever happened to me. After I stopped hating him for dying and leaving me I noticed this. I can't help wondering what would have happened to us if we were still together. Would we still be together? Would we have got married the moment I was sixteen? Now that he has gone, I have to find my life again, and leave his where it was supposed to end.

I have got to that stage where I can let go. I can let him rest in peace. To the people that loved him, though, his death is still alive in their minds. His mother, Phoebe, blames herself, and has had severe depression since he died. His brother tried to take his own life last year. His father has always tried to keep the family together. When I knew him, he was the one who was never around. I realise that he is actually the strongest one of the whole family. Trying to make them happy is the first thing on his mind. I admire his courage.

How I Met My Dream Man

Amy Pragnell

How I Met My Dream Man

All this started only a month ago. I remember it like it was only yesterday. I know that sounds like a horrific cliché, but since this all began my grip on time has been getting a little – how shall I put it? – woozy. And could you blame me? This kind of thing doesn't normally happen to your average teenager – especially the average teenager whose grades are considerably less-than-average and is currently experiencing Exam Panic. When I saw the psychiatrist and told her what I'm about to tell you, she attributed it to stress. My mates thought I was going nutty – I hope this proves that I'm not.

OK, I'm getting a little bit ahead of myself. I'll start at the beginning, which was at about half past two on a Sunday morning – the kind of time anyone with school the next day is usually asleep. Like I was.

I was having a pretty normal dream – you know, fall down a black hole, get chased by a three-headed Maths teacher and do unmentionable things with a toothbrush – when in the midst of being chased across a flaming bridge I encountered A Someone.

I had no idea who it was (unusual in a dream, because, for some reason you normally know that the polar bear eating a cheese sandwich is really your principal), but I knew before I even focused my dream-eyes on him that he was *seriously* important. I mean, seriously. And when he turned round, in classic movie style, I nearly fell over (in my dream). He was – how shall I put this without sounding crass? – unimaginably beautiful. Beautiful is normally a pretty girlish kind of good-looking, and in a way he was. I couldn't really focus on the details, but I didn't need to. He had unreal eyes . . . the lashes were even longer and heavier than mine, and the irises were an indescribable shade of green, flecked with tiny stars of silver and gold light that seemed to come from inside him. Emeralds had nothing on them. They were the most expressive eyes I'd ever seen. And all he did was to say: 'Talli'.

I always thought my name sounded stupid, but spoken by him it took on a million meanings. Unfortunately, that night, all I got to hear was my name, before the alarm-clock went off and woke me up. I never hated that clock so much before in my entire life.

I walked around all day with a stupid grin on my face, according to my best friend Shola. She insisted that I looked like a cat that had got the cream and when I protested that I hadn't done anything the night before she stood on the roof of the bike-shed and started shouting that I was in love.

She was right. A single word by a non-existent

person in a dream had reduced me to the worst kind of quivering, love-sick fool. But that wasn't the worst of it. Oh, no.

I fell asleep in class for the first time in my life.

I was watching Miss Guise-Smith writing up key words in the reproductive cycle of amoebas, with a considerable degree of boredom, when my eyelids began to droop. Before I could actually drop off (or so I thought), I spotted what looked like a new boy being led into the room by Mr Finnely, the principal. He introduced the boy as Chaser – no surname – and Miss Guise-Smith sat him in the seat next to me. Within seconds he had leaned over and passed me a note. *I've been watching you. You're special.*

Normally I'd write back and call him an inconsiderate pervert, but as he passed the note I'd seen his eyes, and they were several shades of emerald green. But before I could say anything to him I felt some serious pressure on my shoulder, and was shaken awake by Shola to the sneers and sniggers of my classmates, and the sarcastic remarks and detention provided by Miss Guise-Smith. MORTIFICATION!

My parents were out again when I got home. I was meant to do my homework, but somehow I found myself sitting, not in my bedroom, but in a room in our house I'd never encountered before. It looked like a Victorian study. I was about to start being nosy, looking at the books on the shelves and poking around in drawers, when the door opened and in walked *him* – Chaser.

'Talli,' he said, in the voice that made me go weak at the knees and my mouth try to hang open. 'Can I talk to you?' I got a full stare from the emerald eyes and I had absolutely no will of my own. I was his puppet.

He talked for *hours*. He talked about waterfalls, art, politics, angels, sunrises, planets so far away that it took a lifetime-and-a-half just to reach them, famous people and works of literature . . . and as he spoke I could see them in front of me. I was *furious* when something warm and heavy landed on my lap and stuck its claws into my leg, forcing me to wake up and feed the cat – at three a.m.

The next morning I found I'd overslept – and I was absolutely shattered. I could barely keep my eyes open as I stumbled into tutorial and stared blearily at the board. Shola whispered something to me about being kept busy by loverboy last night, but I couldn't get my mouth connected to my brain and just shook my head.

I must have shaken my head while Mr Jackson was asking a question, because he gave me a detention, kicked me out of the classroom and told me to go and see Mr Finnely.

I wandered into the office and waited for Mr Finnely to say something. He looked up from one of his many bits of paper (the ones that floated around his office for days before he got around to reading them) and scowled at me from underneath his killer eyebrows.

'I hear you fell asleep in class yesterday,' he snarled.

'Yes?'

'Do you think it might be a good idea to go to bed *before* midnight tonight, so that you aren't so tired for tomorrow's lessons?' he asked sarcastically.

I decided to ignore the sarcasm and try to be honest for once in my life. 'I went to sleep about five minutes after I got in from school yesterday,' I said, trying not to glare at him, because I've been given detentions a-plenty for 'eyeballing' members of staff. I've been given them for 'back-chatting', too.

I got two detentions from that little interview – one for back-chatting, and one for lying to the principal. Sometimes there's just no way to win.

I got back to the classroom and doodled all over the back of my file. Shola leaned over my shoulder about five minutes before the end of the lesson and whispered to me, 'Talli, you're weirding out. Why the hell have you drawn, like, fifty million eyes and written "I love Chaser" all over that? And who the hell is Chaser?'

I really began wondering why I was ever best friends with Shola in the first place, before remembering that it was because being Shola's best friend was the highest social standing you could get in our school. Right at that moment I thought that social standing had nothing over having a decent friend who didn't criticise your moments of complete and utter infatuation with non-existent people.

And where on earth do you find a friend like that?

In the end, the only person I spoke to that evening before going to sleep at *six thirty* was my cat, Boogie Down. Sometimes I really think that cats are probably the only things on this planet that make sense.

I was only asleep for about two seconds before Chaser arrived. He gave me one soulful look with his amazing green eyes that spoke gallons. Deep and meaningful was obviously the order of that night, along with monosyllabism. He didn't say a single word, but I understood him all the same. We ran through the whole of the Sahara Desert – just for the hell of it. And I was *just* on the point of kissing *the* most perfect man in the universe (Chaser) when the phone rang to inform me that Sunni-glass Double-Glazing was making an early call – eight in the morning! – to ask if I was interested in buying double-glazing.

The sales rep was left with the distinct impression that I didn't. Loudly.

As days went by I got progressively worse – I was falling asleep in every class, on the bus, at dinner, in the shower, though occasionally I actually made it to bed without falling asleep on the stairs.

My parents wanted me to be checked at the hospital for narcolepsy, but I thought it might be a good idea to explain to them *why* I spent so much of my time asleep.

Big mistake. Huge. My mother patted me *very* gently on the arm and said in a talking-to-idiots-or-violently-insane-people voice, 'They're only dreams, Talli. They're not real.'

So I lost my temper and locked myself in the bathroom where – guess what? – I promptly fell asleep and went water-skiing with Chaser, followed by sunbathing in the Caribbean.

My parents' next move was to send me to the psychiatrist I mentioned. Dr Lesley Wheldon was pretty sympathetic about it, and when I explained that I knew perfectly well that they were dreams (I couldn't bring myself to say 'only' dreams), she began writing a little note to the effect that there was nothing wrong with my mental health.

And then I saw Chaser behind her, bold as brass and grinning at me over the doctor's shoulder. He pointed to the doctor, laughed at her and mouthed the words, 'I love you.'

And then he pointed at Dr Wheldon again and added, 'Tell her I'm here.'

And so, obediently, I did.

Nothing really changes here, but it doesn't matter because I can leave my cell with Chaser any time I want. The staff here keep trying to feed me anti-psychotic pills, but I think they've established that I'm not really a threat to anyone. Last time I saw Chaser we went sky-surfing – you know, where you tie a surfboard to your feet, put a parachute on your back and jump out of an aeroplane? – and that was a lot of fun.

According to the head doctor here, I sleep about eighteen to nineteen hours a day. I tell him that it's more interesting than being awake, and he just sighs and goes off to talk to the nurses. When he comes back he often says something like, 'I know you think life is boring, Talli, but remember that it's more interesting outside.' Just saying 'Outside *what*?' usually gets rid of him – he goes off in a temper. But I don't care. I've got my dream man, and I'm happy.

The Last Summer Girl

Rebecca Prestwich

The Last Summer Girl

Every summer we went to the island. It was meant to be our chance to get away. It never worked. Wherever my mother went she took the city with her. Phones, faxes, piles of documents, all sent parcel post to our beach house weeks in advance. 'Just in case,' she'd promise. I gave up listening to her promises when I was seven.

I tried not to let her get to me. The island was too magical and the eight weeks I spent there too short for me to waste. The violent green sea swept away my insecurities, took them swirling away from me, dancing down the deserted beach. My silent fantasies rang out around the shaded woods and echoed off the mountains. Every morning I woke up dizzy, cicadas singing in my ears, lost inside myself. On my enchanted island.

I got lonely sometimes. I grew up on those holidays and I had no one to share it with. I never knew the other kids. Crowds of shrieking teenagers, giggly girls and boys with backwards caps. Then, at the centre of it all, there was always him. You couldn't help but notice Joe. Even as a kid there was something different about him. In his eyes, like a caged lion, angry but sad, daring you to laugh at him. And in his smile, that broad, open grin, always there to hide everything. It never slipped, but everyone knew that there was danger behind it.

It was Mr Johnson, the greengrocer, that I first asked about Joe. I was eleven at the time. Joe can't have been more than thirteen himself, but he already seemed distant and untouchable. I didn't even know his name. Joe Samson was definitely a taboo subject. All I knew was that he had no mother, and he was always in trouble. I still remember the day I asked. Seventy years later and I remember every word.

'Excuse me, sir,' I said. 'Can I ask you something?'

' 'Course you can, Katie doll.'

'Mr Johnson, who's that boy?'

'What boy, love?' he answered, knowing exactly who I meant.

'You know . . .' I whined. 'The Samson boy? Why's he only here in the summer? Why doesn't he live with his father?'

'See, Joe Samson, he has problems inside his head. He goes to a special school, off the island, so as they can sort him out.'

He made it sound simple. Problems, inside his head. You couldn't blame him. His mother had been a show jumper, all sorts of trophies and her face in *Hello*. They say Joe would have been trained to go the same way. But when he was little there was an accident, a car crash. They found them hours later. Silhouetted against the evening sky, the mangled shell of her car, blood on stones and Joe clinging to the cold body of his mother.

You couldn't blame him, but things went from bad to worse. He couldn't be a naughty kid for ever. He had to grow up.

I was there the summer that he got the motorbike. He was only fifteen. The islanders were up in arms. His dad didn't notice. Mr Samson was a broken shell of a man. Turned to drink and ignored everybody. Never noticed if Joe was there or not. And at night you could hear him. Howling at the moon.

That was the summer it started to change. The summer girls started. Clinging to the back of his bike, pretty and laughing, their long hair billowing behind them. I envied them so much; I wanted to be one of his summer girls. It was my dream. But dreams can't be real.

It happened by accident. I stumbled across him in the woods. I was seventeen, and I could go wherever I wanted, my mother had long since given up worrying about where I was. He was perched on a fallen tree, a half-empty vodka bottle resting at his feet. The sun shone down on his swiftly-twitching hands as he rolled a cigarette. It was a typical island day. Clear and sunny, a light breeze whistling around the woodland, rustling the leaves and keeping control of the oppressive heat. I lingered in the shadows, watching him. His eyes were fixed, concentrated on something I couldn't see.

'Kathryn, innit? You own that big posh house by the beach.'

He spun round so he could see me. I felt my cheeks on fire.

'I've seen you around. You have very pretty eyes.'

'I saw a play once. This girl said that blokes only tell you that you've got pretty hair or eyes if you aren't actually that attractive.'

I still don't know why I said it. He tossed his head back and roared with uncontrollable laughter.

'Jesus! You don't get many compliments, do you? Most girls would giggle, at least smile, say thank you.' He paused. 'But then, maybe you aren't most girls.'

He had the most striking eyes. Vivid, violent blue. I could feel them piercing right through me. Overcome with shyness I turned to go, but he called me back. He was drunk. He normally was. But not so drunk he didn't know what he was doing. He could always see straight.

'You're not rushing off already, are you, my favourite little rich girl?'

'Favourite? How many have you got?'

'As many as will have me!' He grinned.

He was finished with the special school now. Finished with school altogether. He was nineteen, nearly a grown man and a permanent resident on the island, but he still had his summer girls, and this year was my year.

Joanne's party was going to be the biggest event of the year, see summer in with a bang. I was part way through my holiday, four weeks gone and another four to come, but for the others summer was just starting.

He was over half an hour late to pick me up. I stood twitching my curtains, peering anxiously down the drive. The sky was a deep, dangerous colour, almost indigo, and scattered with black clouds. It was too hot, airless. My dress clung to my back. I was damp with sweat. We'd picked out the dress together, on the mainland. It was soft, like crushed velvet, shades of purple dripping into each other. He'd sneaked into the changing rooms to watch me try it on, arched his eyebrows teasingly as I shrank away from his gaze. The shop assistant stumbled in on us entwined in each other and hurriedly ushered us out. We hung around just long enough to pay for the dress. That afternoon we ran to catch the last boat home, then sat for hours in the sand, watching the sea, not speaking, just breathing each other in.

I heard the bike on the gravel and scampered out to meet him. My mum would have gone mad if she had seen me on it, but she never did. In a way I wanted her to. I preferred it when she was shouting, angry – at least that showed she cared. Anything would have been better than her total indifference to everything I did.

'You all right, Kat?' he called above the roar of the engine.

I climbed on and clung to him. I wasn't scared, but still I hung close, to feel his warmth next to me. I loved riding that bike, watching the envy in little girls' eyes as we tore up the island, feeling the rush of wind in my hair. It was how I imagined my life would be like: behind me, spiralling clouds of dust, fading into nothing, and in front, only Joe, and miles of open road.

We were late to Joanne's. We were always late, Joe and I. He said he hated the start of parties. I wouldn't know. The only parties I went to were with him.

It was a beach barbecue. Music blasted out from loudspeakers scattered across the sand. The music was fast and furious, catchy anthems with the same lyrics skipping and circling round and round. As we arrived crowds of people ran towards us, out-stretched arms offering us a drink each. They were squealing and laughing, stumbling in the hot sand, their voices high with excitement. Pathetic really, the way they all flocked to him. So eager to please, so desperate to impress him. But it didn't seem that way then, back when a twitching eyebrow or a lopsided grin was enough to set your heart on fire. He was always the star attraction. I could almost see Joanne scrawling it across the invitations, *PS Joe will be there.* I remember dancing on the beach, holding tight and clinging on to save ourselves from sinking into the sand. I stumbled a beat behind, waiting for the pounding rhythm to flow through his hips and into me. I hung my head backwards, laughing, dizzy with the heat and him. We were all dripping with sweat, hot and clammy. Everyone cheered as the skies broke open and the rain came down, drenching us. We lifted our arms and tilted our faces, dancing with new energy, invigorated by the storm.

We were staggering further down the beach to find a drink when I heard them calling him. He looked reluctant for a minute, but I tugged at his hand and he followed. It turned out that they were lighting bombs in empty brandy bottles and dashing them out into the sea. One boy, Oliver, juggled them two at a time. Tossed them out to sea, seconds before they exploded. Joe wasn't watching the bottles. He was staring at the crowd, watching how their faces, which were illuminated by the flames, were filled with admiration. Suddenly he laughed, scornfully.

'You reckon that's good?' he scoffed, stepping forwards.

I touched his arm. He smiled down at me.

'It's all right, babe,' he whispered. 'Easy, in this

73

rain.' To the crowd he called, 'I'm going to give you a whole new definition of good.'

He skidded on the wet sand, grinning as he regained his balance. He turned to face his audience. Silently he lit the bomb and hurled it high into the violent sky. Orange flames leaped and swirled, spitting and snarling against the darkness. He spun round twice and, without hesitating, he held out his hands. Ready to catch it.

It should have been spectacular. I don't know what went wrong. I remember the rain pounding down on us, waves crashing against the beach, and the wind whipping up the skirt of my dress, dancing around my bare legs. I remember sirens, screams, flashing lights. I remember the rain kept coming, and as the ambulance rolled away, I couldn't tell the rain from my tears.

He wasn't in hospital long. The day he came out summer was still in bloom. Three days before I had to go home, the sand was still hot under my toes. I saw him standing, staring out to sea and I was so happy, he was there the same as always. The sun was still shining on my enchanted island, and I ran like a little girl, tripping and falling towards him. I called out to him, my voice rising with enthusiasm.

'Joe! Joe!' I said his name again and again, still skipping out to him. And then he turned around.

His face was twisted, contorted. His right profile was

as strong and handsome as always, but his left . . . In patches the skin was raw and red, stretched tight across his fragmented features. In others it puckered and folded, sagging under his eye.

'You know, Kat, when you aren't really attractive people tell you how pretty your eyes are.'

It was true. In his sharp blue eyes there remained a cruel beauty, a constant reminder of what he once was. They shone out from beneath the gnarled, dishevelled skin. I turned away from his stare, afraid he could see into my soul.

When Joe was twenty-five his father died in suspicious circumstances. They say that Joe killed him, that after the accident his soul grew as twisted as his features.

He locked himself away into his own private life, away from cold comfort and prying eyes. Who knows what went on in that distorted mind. Still, I don't believe it. I remember another Joe. A tender, loving Joe, who held my hand and laughed at my shy smile. A wide-eyed, laughing Joe, with lion's eyes and daggers in his smile. My Joe tried to kill himself, days after his father died. He was taken to an institution, away from the island. Every year I go back there, and every year I look for him. My island has lost its enchantment. The dreams which once echoed around deserted woodlands are lost in a host of fairground rides and flashing neon signs. But I still half expect things to go back to what they once were. Behind the clutter of ice-cream kiosks and souvenir stalls I still half expect to see him, a powerful profile staring out to sea.

I got married. It didn't last long. Paul, my husband, grew tired of 'playing second fiddle to some mutated lunatic', my 'childish and irrational fear of parties' and 'that blasted island'. I'm getting too old to go there now. I'm almost eighty-one and I'm entirely alone.

If only my mother had never taken me to the island. If only he hadn't been in the woods that day. If only we'd gone out alone instead of to Joanne's. If only Oliver couldn't juggle with fire. If only Joe had made that catch. 'If only' are the saddest words in the world. I know I shouldn't be sad for him. Just because something ends doesn't mean it should never have been. After all, even the most beautiful days eventually have their sunsets. Still, I can't help wondering about Joe. I wonder whether he's still alive, and if he is I wonder whether he still wonders about me, his last summer girl.

Red

Sally Roe

Red

Think about the first time little girls wear make-up –
clown circles on their cheeks, bright blue on the eyes
like their mothers way back in the seventies. It's
adorable, the bloody-lipped scrawl, the incongruous
sex of it on their cupid-bow mouths. And they get
used to it too, the pirouetting. It goes with their
Barbie dolls, I suppose.

But the first lipstick I ever owned, when I was
about nine or ten, wasn't red. It was pale pink and
pearlised. I think my mother wanted it to go with my
eyes, that late-seventies doll-face again, or maybe
she was trying to disguise through discretion the fact
that her little girl was growing up, out of the Olilly
dungarees and miniature Doc Martens she'd dressed
me in, escaping into a pink and white world of my
own. Maybe she felt ashamed of my desire to be
some nine-year-old Barbie doll when she wanted me
to be interested in chemistry and physics and maths.
She hadn't fought against the ironing board and gotten
married in a black dress just for the housewife gene
to resurface in me, after all. Really, I was never cut
out for pink, though. I wasn't pretty any more by the
time I was nine: I was already tall, too mousy and thin,
with thick-lensed spectacles. If I look at photographs

of myself then, I wonder why the frames of those glasses were so big. They overlapped the edges of my face and shrank my eyes to little malevolent specks, staring glumly out of a straight fringe or grimacing in forced smiles.

Of course, I wasn't like that. Malevolent, I mean, or even grimacing. I was a long way off feeling ugly, being really too tall and not merely shooting up. But I was nearer to the abject misery of the first years at high school than I realised, that's for sure. Maybe it was some subconscious dread of what was to come that prompted my sloughing-off of pink, almost as quickly as I had buried myself in it, some sort of grim foreboding that I would never be like curly blonde-haired Laura in her ruffled skirt, who drew admiring glances from all the parents (except my mother) at our various birthday parties.

Red shoes. That was much earlier than pink. I must have been about six. In a shoe shop, my mother shaking her head but smiling, not really about to deny me them. She wouldn't let me walk home in them, though – red patent leather slip-on shoes with bows on the toe. For parties, I suppose, though I have no memories of ever wearing them, just trying them on in the shop and walking home listening to the bump of the shoe box against my mother's side. They were fairy shoes, I thought. They made me feel magical, and they were almost certainly the first step in red's gradual seduction of me.

High school. The uniform top was a peculiar bright, almost jade, green – an unnatural colour, my Art teacher says. The polar opposite of red. Maybe it was precocious anti-establishment tendencies which drove me to my affinity with red over any other colour, then. My father would have been proud. But I didn't choose it for my new bedroom. I insisted on pale purple and magnolia and floral prints. That wallpaper was the last gasp of the Laura inside me who was slowly being strangled by the twist of my stomach every time I walked into a room and it fell silent.

I worshipped red secretly, illicitly. Its symbolism was not lost on me. Red for anger and love, the emotions I floundered my way through for what seemed like for ever, scribbling them out in appalling poetry on red notepaper. I never wore red then. It was too bright for my drabness, the camouflage I had adopted. Although wearing a neon sweatshirt five days a week made it hard to fade into the background, I made a passable stab at it. Whole conversations and intrigues were played out around me. I was so invisible that secret snogs went on in rooms noisily emptied of everyone except me, my head buried in a book until I heard a pubescent slurp, turned round briefly, and then back to the book. By now I really was malevolent. I hated more or less everybody I met with a passion bordering on the pathological.

I dreamed of walking into assembly and gunning them down. Red accompanied me into these dreams like a familiar friend, in the splashes of blood on the parquet floor. It woke me up laughing, but it was a poor consolation. After all, it was me who was gunned down every day by their whispered and not-so-whispered words.

I read my way through the first three years of school. Only my German teacher noticed my copy of *Tess* under the desk, the rest were too busy pulling the lads down off the tables, dodging the mis-split infinitives and more tangible missiles. Some of the boys were already as tall as the teachers, but I was taller. It was a bleak time, but eventually I began to wear bright colours again. Rainbow fishnets, tie-dyed dresses, that recurrent blue eyeshadow. I was loud and obnoxious and ugly outside of school and quiet, obnoxious and ugly inside. That was the general consensus and the narrowed eyes and hissed threats had put me firmly in my place. There was no reason for me to think that my long-term prospects would be any different.

It would be romantic to say that red was to change my life, but it didn't. Contact lenses and sudden breasts did that, but red was more reliable than either. The first was apt to get lost after the first litre of cheap cider on the park bench, and the second I found faintly embarrassing after all the years of anxiously waiting for their arrival. By now my pair of bright red patent leather Doc Martens were my trusty steeds, my Silver. Of course, it didn't last. After a year or so they provoked nothing but a cringing fondness, but back then, aged fourteen, I felt invincible with them on. Clicking my heels together three times never brought me home, wherever that was, but I never stopped hoping that it might.

Red boots, shortly followed by red lipstick at last. In fact, maybe that came first. I remember squinting through my specs to apply it, but I don't think I wore it out of the house before the centimetre-thick veils of glass were lifted from my eyes. It came off on mugs, the ends of biros, my hands, my teeth. By the end of the day it was a faint smear around the very outside rim of each lip. That lipstick was as unreliable as the acne-ridden, bubble-jacketed boyfriends of my more popular peers but I put up with it anyway, just as they tolerated their decidedly un-lovelorn swains. I loved its connotations, or the ones I saw. I had visions of crimson-lipped heroines pacing the moors rather than the tired genitalia on display, or nearly on display, along the top shelf of the newsagents. I wasn't into Freudian stuff, then, remember.

Red didn't mind that I was only fifteen, though. It had no compunction about making me look a slut, smudging bloody crescents on every item of crockery within reach. And I noticed, around then, that I was being noticed. Only sized up, but still noticed. Red screamed, forced me into a spotlight. It wouldn't let me blend into the background. It was only a matter of time before the flowery wallpaper began closing in on me and clashing with the face in my mirror. Almost overnight, I started seeing red everywhere. We met at postboxes, traffic lights, in the art galleries we visited with school. Red underwear clutched me for a day until I banished it to the back of the drawer. I think I felt it was moving too fast. I still wanted the romance, the courtship of shop windows and make-up counters, the red paper that began to receive increasingly obsessive missives dedicated to blissfully unaware boys.

And what happened to my parents in all of this? It had the same effect as any first serious teenage relationship. Red gradually eased me away from them, became the newly-dominant influence. My mother thought that red lipstick was a bit tarty and she had a phobia of red nails dating from a childhood fear of a wicked witch in some Disney film or other. My father, after grandly proclaiming, when I was still about eleven and ever so respectable-looking, that he would never argue with me about my appearance (once more the liberal parent) bit his lip harder and harder as I tottered out and staggered back through the door, wearing thinner, shorter and more trans-parent layers of clothing. I stained his underwear cerise with a misjudged load of washing and spilled maroon nail polish on my bedroom carpet. No wonder things between us were somewhat strained for several years. But I refused to believe that my talismanic make-up would attract the wrong sort of attention, and even when the catcalls and free drinks it conjured up with increasing frequency eventually persuaded me that it was a distinct possibility after all, I refused to let it scare me off. We were inseparable.

The first time I dyed my hair was an attempt at red but it came out as a 'natural' red, which translates as ginger. It took me several years of moving through the spectrum: blues, purples, black and platinum blonde, before I finally returned to the beginning. I got it right this time. Scarlet, like the inside of a Fabergé egg. It was the first time I realised that red could let me down, and I never really recovered from the shock. It made me look so pale that my face was a ghost's face underneath a scarlet mop. Black lipstick transformed me into a warped Snow White until after a few weeks I decided that red and I would have to go our separate ways for a while. I didn't mean for that to be the end of it, though. I bought another pair of red shoes as a conciliatory gesture a few weeks later, velvet sandals with stacked soles, but I never wore them. Like all the most well-meaning gestures, it went horribly wrong. The three-inch heels crippled me and suddenly I realised I no longer wanted to act the willing geisha. I abandoned the lipstick as impractical – smears on my chin were a warning to my mother that my late arrival home wasn't because I had missed the bus. My red notepaper ran out and a year later I threw away the poems. It sounds clichéd, but gradually we just drifted apart.

I threw myself headlong into new 'relationships', drunken fumblings initiated in cheap, dark clubs and alleyways. Well, perhaps not alleyways, then, but those clubs were just as sordid. It was a rebound thing, I guess, but the various boyfriends never seemed to live up to their predecessor. I found it impossible to become as obsessive about them as I had been about red, and I found two-sided conversations much harder going than my impassioned, written monologues. Lapsing into silence didn't really help, either – they were too quick to interpret it as the sort of thoughtful intelligence I'd dispensed with as a social liability some years earlier. Nevertheless I gained a reputation for being a good listener, an all-purpose roll of Andrex for those private-school puppy dogs who littered the student pubs wearing record bags and soulful expressions. Once they'd figured out the limited extent of my compassion, it was often too late to save themselves, and after a few of these unsatisfactory dalliances in quick succession, being a good listener wasn't the only reputation that started to precede me. It was my own fault, though.

I took to the blonde standard of low-cut tops and trivial conversation like the proverbial duck to water, learned how to bat my eyelashes and never wondered why I couldn't be bothered doing anything else. I realised that somehow along the line I'd managed to attain the status I'd envied Laura so bitterly for, stepped straight into her shoes, in fact, but it was a pretty hollow victory. Even once I'd learned how to talk in whole sentences again and stopped flinching whenever I made eye contact with a stranger, once I'd got pretty good at pretending, part of me was always yearning, wanting for something. I could never remember exactly what.

But I don't suppose you ever totally forget your first love, and red was definitely mine, waiting just beneath my subconscious. Pink was just a crush, shrugged off at an early age, but red was truly an object of adoration, the real thing. Analysts would have had a field day. Red as a projection of a young girl's awakening sexuality. Well, could you blame me? Have you seen a fourteen-year-old boy recently? Once they started washing more and spitting less, red lost its potency, its power. I suppose lust was no longer something to be deified, once it began to be realised.

And last week, in town, I saw it. Red, scarlet, crimson, all sequinned and gorgeous and utterly impractical. On the hanger, it promised to turn me into Marilyn. On me, thoughts of idols were forgotten. But I bought it and wore it once, for old time's sake. I didn't wear the lipstick, though. I wanted red to know who was boss, that I was a nice girl, anyway, and that I didn't do that sort of thing any more.

It's too soon to say, really, whether we'll stay together this time. Deep down, though, I know that red will have the last laugh. Once I start getting old and desperate, hosting my own parties and plastering over the wrinkles on my face. Red will show up the tiredness in my eyes, the creases in my lips. I'm dispensable, you see. Once I no longer suit red it will stop wearing me.

Out Of Order

Freya Scott

Out Of Order

The following is taken from old newspapers I found in our attic.

The newspapers were yellow with age. He flicked through them. Headlines caught his attention. 'Half the world's population wiped out.' 'Disease kills millions, figures rising.' 'Scientists work day and night to produce clones to replace the dead.' 'Risk of human extinction.' 'Scientists find way to make clones outside the womb. No more labour and pain or pregnancy. Using special conditions to create womb effect.' He looked at the date at the top left-hand corner. March 3rd 2250, seventy years ago.

He turned to another pile. 'Couple killed after having natural-born baby.' 'Couple produce freak.' There were pictures of different couples just before execution.

He eyed the two remaining piles, feeling guilty of intrusion. But his curiosity won him over. 'Inhuman children.' He read through the article, intrigued. 'Cloned babies born feeling no love. All the babies constructed after the Halin disease feel no love. They cannot love.' He wondered what love was and thought about finding a dictionary. He found he couldn't be bothered and carried on to the next newspaper. 'The construction of babies since the discovery has stopped completely.' He stopped and went on to the next paper. The date was 2270. 'Population decline is becoming increasingly worrying. More clones need to be made, but scientists still haven't found a way to make clones love again. Many operations and experiments are being carried out.'

He turned to another newspaper, engrossed. 'Cloning continues at last. The population decline is so extreme that scientists are continuing to clone children who cannot love. Experiments continue.'

He went on to the next pile. It was just about the breaking down of the immune system. He wasn't really interested. He hated thinking about anything to do with his body.

The word love kept coming up. It seemed to be a key word, so he ransacked his bedroom to find a dictionary. He eventually found one. He looked up the word but to his surprise it wasn't there. He tidied up the room so that no one would know he'd ever been up there, then went downstairs for lunch.

'There you are, Benji! You're late,' his helper greeted him.

'Kate, what are you doing?' Patricia asked.

'Nothing.' Kate dragged her stare from the white wall. 'Is lunch nearly ready?'

'Yeah. I came to get you. It's your favourite! Mashed potatoes.' Kate felt sick. But she sat down obediently and forced herself to eat it.

'I've been meaning to tell you,' began Patricia. 'I've found you somewhere to stay this summer, 'cause you know that me and John are going away and I don't like to leave you by yourself. An old friend of your mother's son's place. He lives with his helper.' (Kate didn't know why they didn't just call them robots.)

'Thanks, it sounds great!' Kate tried to sound enthusiastic, as she felt her food coming back up her throat. She rushed to the toilet where she was sick.

'Can you keep it down in there? We're trying to eat!' John said. Kate heard mutterings from him to Patricia. 'Thank God she'll be gone in a few days!' Kate was glad too.

She arrived late. Patricia had taken ages to get the air car ready. Then it had broken down on the flyway. But they had finally arrived. They stood at a large house of grey concrete.

'Now I'll come and fetch you for your match in a couple of weeks, OK?'

'Who?' Kate felt blank.

'You know, the man who you are going to marry? The one that the scientists have matched with you to become good parents for the clone?' Patricia said sarcastically. Another thing that Kate didn't like about the 'community'. Everyone was matched up. Kate pressed the doorbell.

The door was answered by a tall thin man wearing clothes three sizes too big. Wow, Kate thought.

'Hi, are you Kate? I'm Benji.'

'Hi.'

They stood for a few moments, staring and taking each other in. His cold blue eyes seemed distant yet intense.

'Sorry. Would you like to come in?' he asked, moving so there was space for her to push past into the house.

'Yeah. Bye, Patricia, I'll see you in a few weeks.' Kate looked briefly back at Patricia once, before squeezing past Benji into the large hallway behind. She seemed to be lured into the strange building.

'Wow. Nice place,' Kate said, trying to make small talk.

'Thanks.' He didn't seem to be interested. 'Do you want to follow me?' He walked off into the shadows. There were no windows that weren't curtained in the hallway and there were no lights on. Kate had to run after him before his figure dissolved completely into the dust.

They arrived in a kitchen that was very old-fashioned. It still had a microwave and an oven! It was a complete surprise to find a group of young men sitting around a long table, drinking some drink that Kate couldn't make out. 'Hi,' was the general greeting.

She was offered a seat, she took it.

One of the men said, 'I'm Jai, by the way.'

Kate smiled.

'Do you want a drink?' Benji asked.

'Yeah, what have you got?'

'Altst,' he said.

'What?' Kate raised her eyebrows.

'It's an alcoholic drink,' Jai explained.

'Oh, right.' Kate was none the wiser. 'Yeah, why not?' She might as well try it, she thought. She was passed a bottle of something. Everyone else seemed to be drinking from the bottle, so she did too. As soon as she took a mouthful she spat it out again. 'That's sick.'

Benji and Jai smiled at each other as though they shared a private joke. 'I'll get you some water.' Jai got up and typed 'water' into the food pad. A bottle of water was ejected from the hole in the wall. It was quite modern compared to the rest of the kitchen.

They were quite interesting people: Benji had lived around the world and had many different stories to tell, Jai had had a strange childhood that he didn't want to talk about, but occasionally made a few jokes that weren't jokes. But they would always every so often look meaningfully at each other.

That night they had supper, just Kate and Benji. The others all had to go home. Even Jai, it appeared, had somewhere to go. 'So what would you like for supper?' he asked.

'I don't mind.' Benji just looked at her. 'Pasta would be nice,' she said, after realising that she wasn't being helpful.

'Cool.' He typed into the pad and the food appeared. He handed it to her. She smiled gratefully.

'Thanks,' she said.

The next morning Kate was woken by the beautiful sound of someone playing the piano. She got dressed and went to investigate. It seemed to be coming from behind a pair of large doors. She opened one cautiously and peered round. Across a huge room, large enough to fit an army into, she thought – well maybe not that big – she saw Benji sitting at a large grand piano with a cigarette hanging out of the corner of his mouth.

Kate noticed plain white walls, except for a mirror overhanging a fireplace, but that and the piano were the only things in the room.

'Sorry. Did I wake you?' he asked, not looking up.

'Yes. It's beautiful. I've never heard anyone play like that before. You seem to make it come more alive.'

He looked up that time and smiled. 'Thanks.'

She walked over to him and looked down into his cup of cold coffee. It was filled with cigarette butts and ash.

'That's revolting.' She took the cup through to the kitchen and threw it in the bin. Benji finished the piece and followed her. 'I thought your helper lived here. I haven't seen her around, though.'

'Who? Oh, you mean the robot. I gave it a holiday.'

Kate looked at the walls as the kettle boiled. These, unlike the others, were covered in paintings and photographs.

'Did you do these?'

'Yeah.' He sat on the work surface, surveying the room as if it were new to him. Then he got up and went over to an old school photograph. 'Our mothers were friends in school, right? So your mum's picture will be here. What was her name?'

'Maria Thompson.' Kate went forward to look with him. 'There she is.' Kate recognised at once the cheeky smile that she had adopted.

'That's strange. You look just like her.'

'Why shouldn't I?' Kate was entranced by her mother's happy glance.

'Because you're not related to her. You're just the clone given to your parents to look after.'

'So? We were chemically matched. Do you eat breakfast in this house?' Kate was feeling insecure with Benji staring at her.

'Yeah.' He laughed, knowing full well that she felt uncomfortable.

'You're very artistic, aren't you?' Kate felt better again while Benji was making toast.

'I've been encouraged. My father, when he was alive, used to say something has been lost from art. Something about some disease. I don't know. I never listened very carefully – I was always more interested in drawing his head than in what he was saying. He had a little bald patch which I would spend hours drawing.' Benji smiled to himself. 'But that's enough of getting deep. The toast is ready.' His tone suddenly changed from one of being drowsy to being lively. He was very confusing.

Jai came round again later that day. He looked slightly bemused to find Benji in the hopeless task of trying to teach Kate to play the piano. She seemed to have no co-ordination in her fingers at all.

'Hey. What the hell?' He raised one eyebrow quite efficiently.

'She can't even play C major. It's ridiculous!' Benji laughed. Jai smiled lightly, then lit a cigarette.

'You shouldn't smoke, it's bad for you.' Kate slurred happily.

'Is she pissed?' Jai asked, taking a long drag.

'Just slightly. She decided she did like the Altst after all. Then she drank five bottles.'

'Well, no wonder she can't play the piano. You can't expect everyone to be as good as you.' Jai sat on the hard wooden floor and listened to Benji playing a sweet melody. After a while he got up and went into the kitchen. Kate followed him. There was light streaming from the French window at the far end of the immense space.

'What's the rest of the house like?' Kate asked. 'I haven't had a chance to look around yet.'

'It's all the same. Large rooms that are pretty much empty. Some have big canvases in them that have amazing pictures planned out but not fulfilled. Benji gets bored easily. Others just have a few chairs or a table. The kitchen is the only room lived in, apart from his bedroom, which is just as bad as the rest of it. All it contains is a small double bed, a chair and thousands of books that he's never read and doesn't even want to read. Would you like a drink?' Jai, it turned out, was like Benji. He would be deep one moment and then change the subject completely to something quite ordinary.

'Doesn't he care that we're not listening to him playing?' Kate asked, frowning, her cheeks held tightly.

Jai sighed. 'He doesn't play for us, he plays to mock the purity of the world.' Then he smiled, seeing the confusion on her face. 'Don't worry about it, he's very complicated.'

'So I'm learning.'

Jai handed her a drink of coffee. 'Don't spill it. It's hot.' He took his own and went back to the piano room.

Kate gazed after him in awe. She lived the next few days in awe. Jai and Benji seemed to work in a way different to everyone else, a way that seemed to make more sense. They did things that made them happy, not what they thought was right. But not only that, they seemed to create a kind of warm atmosphere that Kate had never experienced before.

Kate woke this time to hear laughing. 'No, seriously, what did you get?' Jai was saying.

'Read it for yourself . . . see? I told you so.' Benji was laughing again. 'And look, the sun's out. It likes me today.'

Jai was laughing too. 'I can't believe it . . .'

'Can't believe what?' Kate asked, getting an orange juice.

'Benji's exam results. He got them back.' Jai turned back to Benji. 'You didn't go to any lessons, you didn't revise, you go into the exams knowing nothing and you get these.'

Kate took the sheet of paper Jai was looking at incredulously. She stared at it. 'Shit!'

He'd got all A*s.

'It's typical of him.'

'So what did you get?' Benji queried.

Jai waved an unopened envelope in the air.

'Well, open them, then.' Kate was impatient.

He tore open the envelope. 'Err . . . three As, the rest A*s.'

'How come you two are so clever?'

'Genetic modification.'

'That was outlawed,' Kate said. The two of them shrugged. 'Well, let's celebrate.' She got the drinks out and they sat around the long table, joking and laughing. 'Pass us an Altst,' Kate asked.

'Come and get it yourself.' Benji smiled. Kate heaved herself up and walked over to where Benji was sitting with the Altsts. As she leaned over to pick up one Benji pulled her down to sit in his lap and then he kissed her on the mouth. She felt his tongue in her mouth. When he let her go she stood back, surprised.

'What was that, just out of interest?' she asked. She had never experienced anything like it before. She noticed Jai laughing. '*What?*'

'It was a kiss,' Jai said.

'That was *not* a kiss.'

'Actually, it was. It was a proper one that has been lost in the mists of time. Did you know that us three are different from the rest of the world? We are the only three than can love,' said Benji, deciding that now was the moment to tell her.

'Wait a second, what is *love*?'

'Something else that has almost been lost. We are the remainder. It is an affection of the mind that is caused by something that delights, or a strong liking for a person. We can feel emotionally attached to a person. No one else can do this. We are unique.' Benji said it like it was some spiritual reading.

'Is he completely pissed?' Kate turned to Jai.

'No, he's telling the truth.' There was a silence while Kate wondered whether to believe or whether it was some joke they'd thought up between them. 'Think about it. We're different from everyone else. You must have realised that. Well, it's because we are human. Think about it. Did you get upset when your parents died? And everyone else gave you weird looks and asked why. It was because you loved them, but no one else understood that.'

'OK, so how do you two know about that?' Kate challenged them.

'My mum wrote me loads of letters. I found them, and some old newspapers. They told me all about it. I told Jai. All our parents were friends.' Benji and Jai were deadly serious now.

'Shit,' was all she could say.

'So you gonna go to uni?' Benji asked Jai, going from deep to off the point. After that the three of them grew close. For the next two weeks they would just sit and talk, or play the piano, or go into the garden and sunbathe. Kate fell completely in love with Benji and Jai but she was friends with Jai. Benji didn't kiss her again. But she didn't mind.

Normally Benji would be up before Kate but on the day her exam results were due she was up first. She sat and waited for the post. When it came she tore open the envelope. It wasn't all A*s but it was better than she had imagined. All As. She ran into Benji to tell him the news. She stopped short.

Benji sat up and rubbed his eyes. 'Are those your results? What did you get?'

'What's he doing?' Kate pointed to Jai.

'He's sleeping.'

'In your bed?'

'Yeah . . .' Benji woke Jai.

'You're both naked.'

'We're in love . . . We thought you knew.'

'What?' She didn't want to believe it. 'No, you can't be. I thought you loved me. You kissed me. How could you?' She was frantic. She yelled some more, not letting Benji or Jai get a word in. She didn't let him tell her how much he did love her. Then she ran out of the house into the road.

There was a screech of an air car as it braked – then the sound of an engine as it moved off. It shouldn't have been on the road, air cars drive in the air not the road. She died instantly, they said. When

Benji went out to follow her he found her body limp. All he said was: I love you. I love you, over and over, hoping that she could hear, but if she'd died instantly she couldn't have. She would never have realised.

Jai was the next one to go; he became ill. There was no cure. The doctors didn't know what it was. They said they'd never come across it before. An unknown disease . . . Benji stayed with him until he died. It took a week and then he was gone.

Finally Benji was the only one left. He gave himself up. He told the doctors he could love. They fried his brain trying to find out what made this possible. They needed to know so that people could love again. He died in surgery. They hit a vital organ. On his death certificate it said he died from lover failure*. They couldn't know he'd died from a broken heart.

This is what was written, but it must be a typographical error for liver failure.

Cher Journal

Marianka Swain

Cher Journal

Friday, 15th December, 1997

They've been talking for weeks about where they're going to. Lucy's off to New York City. 'The Big Apple,' she says. Anybody would think she was a green-grocer. Grace to Sydney, and Joanna to sunbathe in Costa Rica. I'm not going anywhere, really. It's not like my father's Richard Branson or some millionaire. So we're only going skiing in France. BORING.

It'll take ages to get there, and my 'James Bond meets Ryan Giggs' brother gets carsick, coachsick, seasick. The only sick I get is secret agent-football sick.

But now I have to go and repack. My parents are complaining I'm bringing too much. For heaven's sake, a few cases, backpack, Sony Walkman and cas-settes, and a Sainsbury's bag with a few novels. No one realises I positively have to have it all. After all, a girl needs skiing gear, casual but trendy clothes for hanging around in, some cool party stuff, and a few spare outfits. Doesn't everybody? Besides, my Licensed to Kill brother doesn't mind having things by his feet in the car. My legs are too long and I've got to have my space. My family is so selfish. They want all the room for their boring old luggage.

Luv,
Lydia

Monday 18th December, 1997

Finally, we made it. *Vive la pilules de mal de la route*, or long live carsickness pills, for all you uneducated morons. They meant 007 Junior was only sick once on my 'Friends' rucksack. Rachel's hair isn't quite as cool as it was.

My family is so embarrassing.

'Lydia,' my father says. 'Why don't you ask for that sausage in French? After all, we pay all this money for you to learn French, so you might as well speak it. Come on, don't be shy.'

Yeah, right.

My mother's just as bad, calling me names like 'Petal' and 'Tigger'. And in public, too.

But worst of all is my *Goldfinger* brother Jack. What a nightmare. Why do little boys have to pretend that everything is a Walther PPK gun? It's just so sad.

La maison isn't too bad. A little on the small side, but at least I have my own bedroom. I'm probably one of the only girls who doesn't want to spend the night with James Bond. Tomorrow we start skiing lessons with someone called Monsieur Claudaire. I hope he's cute.

Au revoir,
Lydia

Tuesday 19th December, 1997

What a cool day.

Mum said, 'It is quite cool. Maybe you should put on another jumper.'

Keep up, Mum.

I'm in love with Monsieur Claudaire, France – and almost my family. He is absolutely gorgeous, and I think he likes me too. But let's start at the very beginning, as Julie Andrews would warble.

We had to get up at eight o'clock. This is supposed to be a holiday. Obviously, I wasn't in the best of moods by the time we got to the slopes. And there he was. Monsieur Claudaire. He was wearing this really hot ski suit, which looked great with his dark eyes and hair.

At first I thought I would never get a chance to be with him alone, but I actually did. And on the first day, too.

After we learned the basics, my brother zoomed off by himself, ignoring my parents' feeble cries – 'Be careful!' – and my superfit parents stayed behind to perfect their stopping techniques.

Monsieur Claudaire and I skied off together, but

not quite into the sunset. That would be dumb. We even gazed over the beautiful French mountains. It was just so poetic. Now I know what our English teacher was going on about when she sighed over Hermia and Lysander's divine love.

I even got up the nerve to ask him a question in French. Dad's money paid off, after all. I addressed him as Monsieur Claudaire and he actually smiled at me and asked me to call him Jean Paul. It was totally dreamy – in any language.

For the rest of the afternoon I could only think that now we're on a first-name basis. Everything else was distantly formal. Well, nearly everything. No one could miss my father falling head-over-heels into a tree. It was so embarrassing.

'Crash City,' as my not-so-poetic brother put it.

Maybe this holiday might be OK after all.

Je t'aime!
Lydia

Wednesday 27th December, 1997

My Christmas was completely dull. Mum got all wound up about what stuffing to make. I mean, who really cares? And she fussed about what to give Aunty Jane. It's not like she gives us anything interesting. She certainly didn't give me anything from my Christmas list. What's happened to the spirit of Christmas?

But the best gift of all was Jean Paul asking me out. Well, not exactly, but he said something in French which I think meant: 'I go to the Belle Café with my friends and I'd like to go with you on New Year's Eve.'

I was so excited, I just kept nodding and smiling stupidly like Dougal from 'Father Ted', and saying, '*Oui, oui.*'

I yanked out my black miniskirt and blue Warehouse top, then went for my flared jeans and Gap T-shirt. But, thinking about it, maybe I should go for the tie-dyed skirt and Levi's shirt. Not that I worry about wearing labels, or anything. I hardly brought anything with me, so I have no idea what he'll think of me.

Joyeux Noel, Journal,
Lydia

Tuesday 2nd January, 1998

Quelle disaster! I set off at a quarter to ten for the café. My parents said I could go as long as I got back by eleven thirty, so we could start the new year as a family. Totally nauseating. But if I stayed until midnight, maybe he'd kiss me.

When I got to the café, I looked round for Jean Paul. There he was, my Lysander. I was just about to make my entrance when some French blonde went over to him. I think she's another ski instructor.

He jumped up and cried, 'Helene!' He took her in his arms and kissed her. A real kiss, lasting a long time. But it was my kiss. And my Lysander was being stolen by Helena, just like in Shakespeare. Just like Hermia, I made my exit.

I slipped into my room and tried to find words like 'two-timer' in my French dictionary. Dad came in and looked surprised. 'You're home early. It's good to see you're finally using your dictionary. I was convinced you'd developed an allergy to it.'

I ignored him. I could only find the French word for two-seater, which made me feel even worse.

The door burst open. 'Don't move, I'm armed,' a voice shouted, 'and licensed to kill!'

Even though I wasn't in the mood, I couldn't help smiling.

'Do you want to play Cheat with me?' It was *Diamonds are Forever* and the casino scene, where James Bond gets the girl.

'OK.' What did I have to lose? I'd already lost my guy.

We played Cheat, Rummy, One-eyed Jack and Happy Families. Then my brother offered to cook us supper. He has a limited menu of scrambled eggs, toasted sandwiches and cucumber in vinaigrette. He's also pretty hot at serving ice cream, although a microwave to defrost the ice cream does help. We didn't have a microwave, so we had to make dinner conversation at this point. As the clock struck twelve we all yelled, 'Happy New Year!' and hugged each other.

The next day I ran into Jean Paul on the slopes. Not literally, like Dad would. I couldn't find any suitable French words, so I spoke to him in English.

He looked surprised, then amused and sorry. 'Poor Lydia, you did not understand me, I asked for your advice. I did not ask you out.'

'My advice?'

'Yes. I asked you whether or not I should take Helene out on New Year's Eve, I did not know if this would be too serious.'

Of course, there were no fairies and Lysander never stopped loving me, because he never loved me in the first place.

Still, I suppose this holiday has been pretty cool. Even if Jack did get an AK47 machinegun and Aunty Jane gave me a My Little Pony. My Little Ponies are seriously gross. At least my dad now believes I enjoy French, and I can tell my friends that I met a good-looking French boy on holiday.

Anyway, maybe I can get my parents to take me to Italy next year. I've heard that Italian boys are just the best.

Ciao!
Lydia

Where Is My Happy Ending?

Jason Walsh

Where Is My Happy Ending?

Saturday 16th January, 1999

Dear James,

It's so quiet – there is not a noise to be heard. I am thinking of you – I'm just sitting alone up in my room. I'll remind you of it, briefly. The blue-painted walls are covered with posters of female personalities: successful women. You know I've always had a lot of female role models. They're ambitious – they know what they want – they get it – and they take no nonsense. But now, now I'm smothered by faces, smug faces of women who always get their way. Madonna, Cher, Whitney Houston, Julia Roberts . . . all looking down on me!

I'll lie out on top of the bed. Here, I can escape the glares, and enjoy the view through the glass in the ceiling. The impression above makes it so easy to forget the here and now, and think only of important matters. You feel so far, like a falling star I'm wishing on, in the night sky . . . and if it's wrong to love you, then I simply can't be right. I'd give up everything I have to feel you lying beside me. I'd throw it all away because you mean more to me than life.

Why did you leave? Don't you remember how it

used to be? We had the kind of romance that was so hard to believe . . . I can still feel the sand under my feet and the hot sea breeze, when our bodies embraced beneath the palm trees – we had our first kiss as the sun came up. Those were the days . . . and the nights. How could I forget those nights together? You touched my body so delicately, it felt genuine. Time: it's so frightening, isn't it? It's now been fifteen days and eight lonely hours since Mr Joy packed his bags and left . . . Mr Bitter cannot take his place. But I still feel your presence here. Every night, I wait for you – your ghost haunts my room throughout the night: the ghost of yesterday.

Remember Mum hanging over us in the background? She never did agree with it, she hated us together. I can still recall the things she said about your attitude towards life and relationships; but the fact that you were a few years older than me and already had left school only made matters worse. She's so damn strict and old-fashioned; I think it's because she's so religious. Also, maybe because I am an only child and she is an only parent, she probably feels the need to protect me more. But still, I'm eighteen years old, for Christ's sake!

She found me with a poster of Leonardo DiCaprio under my bed a while back; she said that she found it to be a sin, how I stared at their bodies. 'There was none of that in my day!' she reported. When I told her that other people my age did it too, she just walked out of the room. I remember that stern look on her face . . . almost as if she was looking down on me. You were the one thing that kept me going. I only had to think of you and that austere face became a bad memory.

Her deep voice could be heard shouting from the next room, 'Your problem is that you don't pay enough attention to what is written in the Bible. Try reading Psalm 51.2.' When she had gone, I consulted the Bible. That passage read, 'Wash away all my iniquity and cleanse me from my sin.'

I sometimes wonder if our separation was fate . . . was it God's way of punishing me, of cleansing my sins? Was Mum right, after all?

One person who *has* understood me, and you, is my best friend, Mandy; she believed I'd find the man of my dreams. Lately, *you* have been the only man of *my* dreams. I could see you like you were: your skin was gold from the sun. You had wonderful black hair which lifted gently and fell abruptly in the summer breeze. Your hair was one of your best features – so sensual was the feeling to run my bare fingers through it. Brilliant blue eyes you had and so handsome you were, I was the envy of all the girls. It is everyone's dream, to find that someone with whom they just 'click'.

We met on holiday, last year in Ibiza. You were

mates with Mandy, that's how we were introduced. Do you remember that night at the chalet? It was only a few days after I met you, when I confessed to you and Mandy my secret about why I could never be a parent. This secret I had carried with me for a long time. It took myself a while to realise that I would never have a little 'me' toddling about the house: a child to take to the park, to teach about life and, most of all, to love.

I recall the conversation in Ibiza very well, and the things you said to me to make me feel all right, which I carry with me today. You and Mandy entered the room to find me in a terrible state of mind: 'You look so miserable . . . the tears are in your eyes,' you said. I think I was so pleased just to hear you say these things . . . to know you cared. After all, I had felt drawn towards you from the moment I had set eyes on you. When I first saw you, you were a picture of love; and when you first wrapped your arms around me, I felt love. And, after so long, your love has never felt stronger.

'I know you better than anyone,' swore Mandy. 'Tell me what's wrong, and we'll sort it out right now, together.' I looked up at your face: you were dressed in white trousers with a plain white shirt. You stood tall, in front of the hanging bulb in the room. I could sense that you were as sensitive as I was. You knelt down and quietly asked, 'Hey, what have you got to hide? We all have to face the dark at some time, but with us here, you're bound to come out dancing into the light again. No fear is ever as great as it seems.'

Then I explained everything to both of you, and it was understood. I was quite surprised at your reaction, as you let us become closer. The relationship lasted on through the summer and into the autumn: we were no holiday romance – it was much more than that! We only lived a few miles apart, but it took a holiday in a place thousands of miles away for us to discover each other.

But what's the point of it all? I'm living for a dream, and dreams never cross over to reality. They remain in the imagination until they become memories of what never was. I can't deny it, watching the way you watch her. I don't know her, but I know she's everything you're living for. Oh, love is such a miracle, when Cupid has his arrow aimed at you. What should I do? I'm in love, too. You're the bus I'm waiting for, I'm at the stop where buses rarely pass. I'm going on, but I can't let go. Oh why do I think this way at such a tender age?

You insisted that children didn't matter, and that you never wanted to be a father, anyhow. That was all lies, wasn't it, to make me feel better? Your heart wasn't open, so you had to go. Your exact words were, 'Please, please understand, I'm in love with someone else. What you couldn't give me is the one thing that she can.' So, how could I compete with that? Say goodbye, but not knowing how or when the truth in my whole life began. You don't understand because you'll never know the pain to want the one thing that you haven't got. Look at the distance we have travelled . . . I have become one half of the person that exists as us.

You probably think *you* have had it hard. Well, it hasn't exactly been a bowl of cherries for me. I was the one who went out in public alone, only to find myself surrounded by a thousand fingers suddenly – pointed right at me. Mandy tells me I'm imagining things – that people in my situation always become paranoid – but I'm not so sure. I know that I love you, but you make me hate you. It's been so lonely without you here, and you're on my mind all of the time – I hate you for that.

'Move on,' she says. 'Move on,' they all say. Maybe they're right. We never see it coming, but we know it has to end. You may be gone now, but you have helped me discover who I am; and now I *will* choose to live for what I can give. I can show affection to others, I can make others give to me. A renaissance: a symbol of my faith and who I am. You were my first, and we never said goodbye. But now, I must walk along a road that waits ahead: I mustn't let my heart control my head again. I've learned my lesson now, and I'll make everyone remember me. I don't want your sympathy, or one of God's miracles. You can't change for anyone – I know your reasons why.

Remember I loved Madonna's music? I liked Celine Dion and Whitney Houston's music too, but I idolised Madonna, and still do. Her music has always resembled and expressed my most inner feelings. I'm hearing all her heartfelt ballads in my head now, as I come to the hardest part of the letter.

Goodbye forever.

Luke

Also available from Piccadilly Press, by
LOUISE RENNISON

Sunday 8.00 p.m.
Walking home, I said, "I don't think he's that keen on her. What sort of kiss do you think it was? Was there actual lip contact? Or was it lip to cheek, or lip to corner of mouth?"

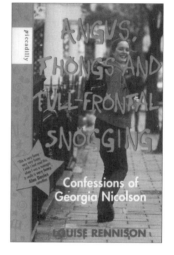

"I think it was lip to corner of mouth, but maybe it was lip to cheek?"

"It wasn't **full-frontal snogging** though, was it?"

"No."

"I think she went for full-frontal and he converted it into lip to corner of mouth . . ."

Saturday 6.58 p.m.
Lindsay was wearing a thong! I don't understand **thongs** – what is the point of them? They just go up your bum, as far as I can tell!

Wednesday 10.30 p.m.
Mrs Next Door complained that **Angus** has been frightening their poodle again. He stalks it. I explained, "Well, he's a Scottish wildcat, that's what they do. They stalk their prey. I have tried to train him but he ate his lead."

*"This is very funny – very, very funny. I wish I had read this when I was a teenager, it really is **very funny**."* Alan Davies

Also available from Piccadilly Press, by
JONATHAN MERES

When Mr, 'hey, call me Dave' Sissons suggests that 5B keep a diary for a whole year, reactions are decidedly mixed! *Yo! Diary!* grants us exclusive access to all areas of six very different fifteen-year-old minds:

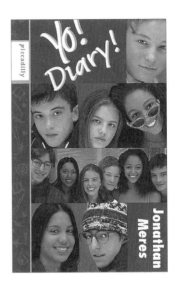

Seb – the rebel and 'Spokesdood for a generation';

Meera – a girl obsessed with astrology;

Steven Stevens – so good his parents named him twice;

Clare – the local neighbourhood Eco Warrior;

Mandy – Ms Personality and Karaoke Queen, and

Craig – convinced that he's the only virgin on the entire planet.

Jonathan Meres has written a riveting and hilarious tale of teenagers teetering on the edge of the millennium! It's a story of changes, drama, love, intrigue and plenty of good old angst! And that's just in the first week!

"Meres' strong, irreverent characterisation and sharp humour (he was a stand-up comedian with his own radio show) make this a book that will achieve an effortless following."
Publishing News

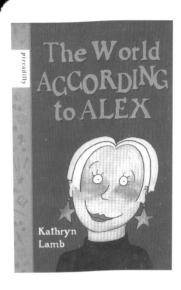

Laetitia Alexandra Rebecca Fitt has more problems than just an odd name. Like three younger brothers (euk!), a baby sister, and an older sister with very strong views on life (Alex's). Having crazily busy parents may mean freedom – which is cool – but it also means they never notice Alex. Added to this, the love of Alex's life (Kevin in Year 12) doesn't know she exists. And then there's friends and parties . . .

By the author of the *Help!* series: *Help! My Family is Driving Me Crazy!*, *Help! My Social Life is a Mess!* and *Help! Let Me Out of Here!* and of the titles *Boywatching!*, *Girls are From Saturn Boys are From Jupiter* and *How to be Completely Cool*.

If you would like more information about the
books available from Piccadilly Press and how
to order them, please contact us at:

Piccadilly Press Ltd.
5 Castle Road
London
NW1 8PR

Tel: 0171 267 4492
Fax: 0171 267 4493